The Arrival of the Old Gods

The Arrival of the Old Gods

Joseph Hopkins

Copyright © 2017 by Joseph Hopkins.

ISBN:	Softcover	978-1-5434-3480-4
	eBook	978-1-5434-3479-8

All rights reserved. No part of this book may be reproduced or transmitted in any form or by any means, electronic or mechanical, including photocopying, recording, or by any information storage and retrieval system, without permission in writing from the copyright owner.

Any people depicted in stock imagery provided by Thinkstock are models, and such images are being used for illustrative purposes only.
Certain stock imagery © Thinkstock.

Print information available on the last page.

Rev. date: 07/05/2017

To order additional copies of this book, contact:
Xlibris
1-888-795-4274
www.Xlibris.com
Orders@Xlibris.com
764418

CONTENTS

The Start of Fear 1
Chaos 2
Endless Life 3
Deep Blue 5
Dream 7
Echo Dreams 9
    Endless 10
Song of Sleep 12
Father's Mistake 13
The Ice Queen 15
The Descent 17
The Quiet 19
The Regret & the Long Dream 21
The Father's Words 23
Long Dream 24
What is Love 25
    Sleeping 26
    The Queen 27
    The Serpent 29
The Beast 31
Happy Wolf Hunt 32
The Madness of a Goddess 33
The Vessel 35
    Walk of Heavens 36
Wedding Day 38
Word of God 39

The Start of Fear

Do you recall the first birth?
Do you hear the call of old?
Tell me mortal what do you fear?
I am the passed, I am what you hear when you sleep.
Do you hear my call?
Do you see the fears of mortals?
It's this place that was forgotten.
This realm Of the passed.
Do not run from me.
I am not hear to kill. Your dears are what keep Me young.
I show you night mares. And give me your screams.
I am so glad to hear them. For all the child
of mortals are so kind to me.
I hear the nightmares and the fears they hold. To walk
the place of old. To hear the cry's of the pass.
Come with me my dear. You will see the realm of the gods.
I wont let you die. I wont let you run. For now you are my
Love.

Chaos

Come one come all and play with me.
I am the god of Chaos.
Join me in the worlds end.
Come let's us end this world.
I am the reason for war's. I am the reason For death.
I am the reason for Chaos.
With out me there is No order.
Now let me help you end your life.
Do run from me. I love the chase.
Send your army at me. Use all of your toys.
Make this fun for me. Prey to your false gods.
And hope they answer.
I will end your plant like I did so many before.
Not end the goddess Of rebirth will save your world.

Prey now. Prey all you want there is no hope for you.
I love the death of all mortals.
No matter what you are I love your Cry's.
The taste the blood in the air.
How wonderful it is.
Mortals all are fun to play with.
Do you want to know why the gods left your plant alone?
Because I Kill her. Her screams were wonderful,
I could not help but to smile so much.
But now it's your plant time to die.
Oh please do run.
For to Night is the last of earth.

Endless Life

I am here. Always here, never dying.

My father told me I was so beautiful.
My mother never look at me.
My sister's always laugh at me the other god's would turn from me.
I never knew what was wrong.
Lock way.

When my father pass my mother lock me away.
I now know what was wrong. I am a monster of Decay.
Trap and alone with this shell. My family left me in this place.
The other god free to do as they wish, I
would always sit and watch the.
Siting and look at this mirror. Am I beautiful. Am I beautiful?
What does one call beauty. I want to know this answer.
Now I am free to walk the plane's of mortals.
What can I find for this word that haunted my thoughts.

I look upon this world of color I see nothing for me.
This place I walk all run from me. The ground I
stand on decay, the people I touch fade away.
Why must I be so alone. This world was to
beautiful. I always ask myself am I beautiful.
I don't know the answer u want. Brother and
sister I ask for you. Come to this place.
What am I the god of. Why do all mortals
flee. Why can't I love like you.

Why can't I hold some one like the rest of you.
Am I just here to pass the time of life and death.
Can I here the voice of the rest?
I can now see a reason now to let you go.
All I wanted was to hold you so.
One part of me will fade the rest of me will stand.
What am I?
Who am I?
I am what Happens to all mortals Death and life Decay.
At the end of your road I am what u wait for. My
life at the start was nothing more then glass.
So much time has pass.
My time to sleep has come. Life and death..Will..Continue.

Deep Blue

Born was I. Lost at sea mother for got all about me.
Deep blue I see the sky,
Never aloud to live above.
Deep blue I see. Lost side me.
What wonder I want to fine above me.
Under this place I live I see so much a ship a boat what do they say.
What sound do this world holds. Forgotten at sea I was for me.
Deep blue my heart is. Alone I always am.
Under this place I see wreck abound.
What are they I ask. Why are they here.
I trust what is not here.
I only wish to see this world.
Deep blue alone with you.
I see something from my cell.
What are they I ask.
They do not look like fish or me.
What are they?
I found one that swims to low. I see it face.
Mortal are like I see. But they are not able to breath.
Deep blue Cell.
My home for all I am.
Trap in here.
The time flows on.

Waters Taste corrupted, No longer clean.
Broken is the place. Shifting waters Taste So bad.
What has happen on the land.
My Cells has open.
I rise to the top to see the light. But what I fine is place of dread.
City all over the land corruption braking the
sky. Water no longer deep with blue.
But black with death of mortal seed.
My mother for got me.
My father trap me. But now I brake this world oceans Over the land.
Flooding this world to make in pure.
I will not stop to I Purify this world.
I will turn this world Deep blue once more.

"Goddess of the Sea Sire."

Dream

Fallow me will you not.
Fallow me to the end.
Fallow the sound.
World has left you now.
Do not worry about me I am at peace.
This place is nice I am not ready to leave.
I am not in pain anymore.
I am free to walk around.
The Roses here Smell so nice, the dark is gone from my sight.
I love this place. The smell is Lovely.
The beauty is my home.
I don't wish to ever return.
I wish to stay in this place.
The flower smell so lovely today.
I don't recall what happen to me.
I wish to dance in this place the voice are gone.
No more darkness.
No more pain.
What did I do to come to this place?
Am I dreaming still.
I love this place. The endless flowers all around me.
Why can't I stop?
I fallen in this world, I Fallen in love with this place.
Is this heaven?
I can not say were I am.
I could be lost in the fade.
What a wonderful place.
Is this my dream to hold?
I love this.

I never been more at peace.
This my fate alone?
I don't mind. This place is quite.
No worry's I have now.
Just the echos of peace.
I want this for so long.
A dream with out pain.
A dream with sleep.
Quite dreams no more pain.
I walk with you all the way.
This path will never fade from me.
I love this place a quite dream nothing let out there for me.
My body gone. My heart still here.
Walk of eternity I will never disappear.
Now I am home a field of rose's
Place of ever ending beauty. I do not wish to ever return.

"Do not forget this long path. Do not forget the heart of the fallen.
Do not let the word's fade away. For a
dream is endless well you sleep."

Echo Dreams

Lost in the cold of Echoes wind. I lost my way too long ago. I lie here in the cold all alone not hearing my voice call out anymore. Do not go do not leave me I will not forgive you if you run from me I may be just cold lying here but I'm still inside the shell., Hollow fragment you would think but I am not I'm just Frozen trapped inside my shell I'm dead I've been dead for a very long time please don't go the fact that you came up with this mountain makes me so happy don't go I don't want you to go.

I will haunt your dreams call your name so you'll never forget who I am. This is what happens when you die so cold. I'll never forget you I always love you but now I wait here so alone so cold. An endless dream when I was alive. It was nice I was happy but now I'm cold I'm empty look up on my face have you forgotten me have you forgotten me no you will not forget me. I will find you while you sleep you'll never know it is me my cold hand on your cheek while you sleep. This is your dream and Nightmare.

I'm still here waiting don't worry I'll bring all of you back to me soon you'll be as cold as me.

Endless

Endless pain in my heart. Darkness that will not part.
Voice of the dark call me home.
The place that I will always call home.
No pain for me always alone.
Do u not see why I run?
I do not hear what yo hear.
My soul is broken my broken heart.
Do not ask why there apart.
My life I been crush.
I have no feel left to give.
But to now I feel a small light.
I do not wish to let it go,
But I know if will never be.
My heart will again bleed.
I will not let this light go.
But my heart will twist again.
I do wonder what this world.
I do not ask anymore.
One friend to another.
I will end.

The soul is Cracked.
One more time I will see.
The light will fade from me.
It will always fade.
A smile will never stay.
The lies in my heart will never fade.
Let me fade way.
Let me find my dream.
Let me find my love.
But I will never find any of it.
My dream will stay a dream
My heart will fade away,
I wish I could just be heartless.

Song of Sleep

Fall to sleep young one. Do not fear the dragon near. The giant sleeps below you. It dreams much like you. That holds no regard for anything while it sleeps. The dragon's breath feels the fires below the city. What sound do you hear when it sleeps? Will the dragon awakes and devours the city or will it sleep. One cannot call what does dragon will do but she will awake hopefully she will not Devour the city. She sleeps and in my Dream sleep sometimes when she wakes periodically she stares at the stars and the beach. Only to fall back to sleep hearing no sound early humans around. Her spirit protects the children while they sleep not the adults only the children. She wants peace for her kind always brings more. Life cycles never change but she dreams always dreams. The dragon's breathe of Fire and Ice she will always wait to hide again. The fire her heart the ice her soul. Some say she's empty but she's not she does have feelings but they're here then. The fire will consume the area around her when she wakes. One can only away for when the dragon returns to see if she'll destroy or protect. This planet was her home before ours. The Mortals destroyed her world and now as she sleeps she feels the pain of this world. The other dragons that sleep will devour this planet but let's hope they do not return.

Father's Mistake

My dear sweet, I never thought it would come to this I lost your mother a long time ago but I will not lose you.

What am I posed to do? You're dying to the same disease that your mother did. Why God why are you taking them for me!

Fuck! You are taking everything from me my life. What does praying get me nothing! I've devoted my whole life to nothing but you. But yet I've got nothing. My wife my daughter both died from same disease. Please God hear me don't let my beautiful daughter die! I devoted my entire life to you. Give Me A Sign help me save my daughter!

Mouths have passed. And my dear daughter has passed away. I kept on praying.. but I never got my answer. Why? Take her from me? I've gone to the church for answers. They give me the same cryptic crap that they always have. I've got tired of waiting for an answer I've cried for the last year.

I can't take it anymore.

I've started going deeper in the madness it's been about 10 years since I buried my wife and daughter. I dream that they're still here my wife's ghost haunts me. My dearest little girl I hear her voice playing in the yard. Yelling daddy daddy come and play on the swings with me Daddy. Why does it haunts me? I've tried to forget about it I've been drowned my sorrows in alcohol. I contemplate holding this gun to my head and all I needed was one bullet. There must be something I can do just to see her one last time. I hear a call. The voice in the Darkness telling me I can see them one last time at least my daughter. Don't worry the voice said to me you would have to do with sacrifice a hundred humans. Do I have to kill them I asked the voice? Yes you do have to kill them but you have to eat their hearts. Contemplating whether or not about this voices deal. Do i devour a hundred human hearts or do I solve my problems. Or do I accept what has happened and Let It Go. I've given in to the weakness I have I want to see my daughter again. So one by one I've gathered up humans. It took sometime but it's done I've gathered up a hundred humans over the last year kill them now I kept them. Poison works wonders when you have friends to help you out. Now is my decision time. Do I eat the hearts for this. . . or do I let then go. I give it into my desire to see her. I started devouring them, you know after the first seven you kind of get used to it. I can't take it anymore I started eating their entire bodies. I don't even recognize myself anymore in the reflection in the mirror. My teeth are sharpen from the bone. Now after consuming all of them I sacrifice my soul to summon her back. Haha it was nice. I give up my Humanity to see you again my beautiful daughter. Was it a mistake that I did this I don't know I have to feed her have to feed myself. Eating peoples not as bad as you think it brings happiness to see her smile. I wonder are we a family again. I can't wait for the next day we'll start consuming the city one person at a time. They call me a monster they called it a mistake call it what you wish. No matter what I've done I'm happy that she's back doesn't matter what you call us before you die all that matters that she smiles. The beautiful little girl that I had so long girl she's back forever together we shall be. We spend so much time together hunting she call me daddy again it makes me happy now. Why I'm telling you this before you die it's because I had my eye on making you my new wife. But first you must die and she's going to kill you when I'm going to watch.

The Ice Queen

What is the point of me being here. Trapped inside this dimension. I remember you father you said I was too dangerous. But I ask myself why? What makes me dangerous he never told me the real reason.

When I was born my power consumed entire solar system. My icy Powers consumed the planets that were around us I was only born out of my father and mother as will. I was not given a choice for my powers. I generally became known icy plague, no matter where they where my power spread like wildfire. Planets Stars we're all consumed by my power. I couldn't bury entire solar system in Frozen Bliss. It was absolutely wonderful. The beauty even the stars were captivating when they're frozen, I often remember seeing the Frozen Beauty that I created. The only reason why stars of Frozen by my power it's my father and mother were both deities. The old God The Dragon King himself. My mother The Rising Phoenix the goddess of fire. My power is very beautiful gift, but yet my father calls me a mistake. Am I really a mistake I love the sound of quiet. Father I really did love the quiet I made all the beautiful ice for you and mother. I know you told me not to kill Mortals but I couldn't resist listening to them scream. It was an accident the first time. But I'd blush the first time made it exciting for screens agonizing pain the cracking of the mortal flesh. How I remember like it was yesterday. The beautiful sounds are there flesh cracking. It was a beautiful sound I danced around their bodies. It was beautiful it was hard not to smile over the sound and the Beautiful Forest that I left there. The Mortals turn to the forest they were the trees. I offered the beautiful garden that I created to my mother and father, my mother looked at me said we're not post to kill Mortals.

Confusion took over me. But why? why must I not kill them why not freeze entire universe? Mortals are disgusting creatures. I tried to make the universe beautiful for you father and mother. Isn't it beautiful all the Frozen world all the dead Mortals it's so quiet now there's no more yelling no more war The Mortals are all gone. . . my father said I did wrong. I thought I did write making a beautiful but empty universe, but they yell at me they told me I was too empty. No emotions but I'm happy there's no more noise. Isn't being happy and emotion?

The past doesn't matter anymore what matter is that I'm trapped. I don't remember how long it's been but I do remember why I'm trapped my father my mother. I will free myself my Talons are left on every world. The snow and ice the cold dead worlds they are mine I will turn this universe into my playground once more. Mother father I will not stop tulip Gods bow before me.

The Descent

I don't know how long it's been here anymore. My memories are all broken where am I now it's quiet here. Was I just dreaming of being free? It's not my fault father, it just happened all I ever wanted to make you happy. Is it so wrong that I like the quiet? I don't recall the reason why I'm here? Where am I why do I feel so empty? This place I'm locked away? But why can I see? I can see people but they're not people they look like Shadows are they what I killed are they my friends?

I've been gone. Am i gone? No I'm lost. I think, what happen were am i? I do not know where I am. It's so quiet here I don't really have much to find. I feel as if I wandered all over the place. The dimension that I'm trapped in is vast I'm not sure where the exit is. What do I do? I feel empty. I want to kill them all. I can hear them screaming can hear them talking. I want them dead, I can still see them stupid Mortals I want them dead. Why can't I kill them why won't they stay dead? Is this all a dream? I could swear I killed them. I want them dead. I clawed my way out. There must be a way to break free they don't deserve to be in this universe. I want to break I will kill your father and mother. You don't think I will I'll find a way my claws are on every world. Just waiting to be released.—Haha-

Do you hear me I'll break free I'll make a beautiful garden. I will devour each and every world that you hold these mortals so dear. I'll destroy your creations for what you've done to me I'll kill all of you no matter how powerful my opponent is or what they are I'll crush them turn them into the beautiful ice. But mother and father I still love you but I will kill you. You put Mortals before me I was your second daughter. But why did you forsaken me? You think that I didn't feel anything. But I do I'll Crush would you create. This universe will return to a frozen graveyard. They will not Escape me. I'll make my own Empire. Over the ashes of your Empire father and mother. But you'll see I'm coming back but I will consume the universe that you created for your little puppets. Don't worry mother and father I still love you.

The Quiet

The freedom the call of the universe beckons me. I don't know what freed me, but I don't care whoever or whatever freed me from my prison I owe them but this universe beckons for the peace and tranquillity of Silence. I'll start my reign and whatever Galaxy that I am in will fall one by one, they all will fall tranquillity will soon be. I will disregard the old gods, I'll disregard my mother and father. For my new Focus is making the universe quiet. The old gods will not care specially the one the one that I love, Yoka the old God of Chaos. My beloved oh how he enjoyed me freezing making everything so lovely. I remember the kind words he said, the screams of The Mortals that's a turn to ice. Oh how it was so lovely now I spread the ice like a slow grasping claws of death. The endless dream of the universe nothing in, the pointless sounds of Mortals The God's creations. Look up on the night sky Mortals watch your stars or planets slowly disappear. The first planet I visit they thought I was a angel, they bow before me I was pleased at first.. but every day that passed drew me more in the madness. As I let out my scream: quiet!: I released my devastating powers instantly freezing the entire continent. It finally quiet the beautiful flowers I just created from The Mortals Corpses, it was devastating lovely. I flick one of mortals body shattering into dust, the beautiful sparkles in the light please my eyes. I love the peace and quiet now but I can still hear Echoes this world's not empty there's still praising me. My Mind Is Made Up This World will be turned into a Crystal Rock. As I float up into the sky I pointed my hand up words creating a flower out of ice, I said to this world you're far too loud it's time that the flower blooms in release my power and the beauty of quietness over this small world goodbye Mortals.

The flower finally bloomed shattering over the planet, the world falls into a deathly silence as a blast of wind and pedals freeze the surface and The Mortals their cities turn to nothing but ice. Do you hear the world is crying another dead and desolate World added to her collection. Slowly one by one planet after planet anything that had a sign of life was turned to ice. She took her sweet time at first, but within a few years she accelerated destroying everything.

The gods did not just take notice they tried to stop her. The four Sons of the High Heavens Royal Guards fought valiantly. The fighting continued for a month, but the queen did not enjoy herself these men were aggravating her. On the final day of the first month she destroyed them all with the blooming flower again annihilating all life in front of her turning them all the Frozen powder. The God cry for the sons lost. She was happy with herself after defeating them, there was nothing stopping her. Remove Force consuming the universe leaving nothing but a cold and lifeless planets behind her.

She did what she wanted to, made the universe quiet. She expected the gods try and stop her, she expected more resistance. As Time passed she wanted the quiet but she pondered to herself.

What have I done, I'm So Alone Now, what to do I do my mother or father have not shown themselves. The other gods have not come. But why? Why do they not show I made a paradise of quiet but I'm sad by it. Could this be what real emotions? Is this what my father was talking about? why do I miss The Mortals? why do I miss them why do I miss them? I do not understand the quiet is all I wanted, and now I just want them back.

The ice queen cried. She tried to figure out why, she could not understand. She asked herself what did she do why did she kill everyone she was pleased but yet, confusion over takes her. Puzzled still trying to figure out what these feelings are she turns to try to find an answer. Searching every place for survivors. Crying out to find an answer, but she still cannot find one. For the universe is empty, and the Gods still have not shown. She cries out loud asking for guidance. But the answer does not come, lost I'm still hoping. Hoping to find her answer. The ice queen drifts into dark slumber. "A long sleep for her. Now we wait."

The Regret & the Long Dream

Mother father I am sorry I did not mean to destroy the universe, I didn't mean it I swear please forgive me. Mother why have you not come and find me? Why why I am still lost. Am I forever trapped in this dream. Why why can't I be free? Mother father please forgive me I did not mean to destroy the universe. I still hear the screams, please make them stop. How long has it been! When was the last time I could see my mother and father? I'm sorry mother father please find me. I wish to see the world again I wish to be forgiven by the others. Please find me I want to be free! Let me out let me go please forgive me! I wish I did not kill them. I don't understand why, what is wrong with me was I created to be a monster? What was my purpose? You always told me father that every son or daughter of an old God has a purpose, but what was mine?

All I see now well I sleep here is The Mortals I killed. The beauty of the Frozen lifeless bodies still screaming. It was a slow process the cold devouring them, at that point I did not realize, The Mortals where your children as well. I regret killing them. I really do I see and hear it all their voices. Every species every planet that I consume. Their souls are added to the place that I call home now. It was not an accident that I destroyed them. I really thought that the quiet is what the gods wanted. the others never tried to stop me. Mother and father you never tried to stop me, father you could have put me in my place mother you could have talked to me and told me what the gods wanted. But I didn't get any advice, I would like to see the universe once more, I don't know how long I've been asleep. This dream of everything dying again. It haunts me, I cry so much for the ones that I've killed. I do not know why anymore I wanted them all gone, but here I Cry For The Mortals. I remember what you said before father one day I'll understand. I do understand now that it wasn't my place to kill The Mortals. I let my discuss with them overtake my judgement, but I'm ready to wake up. Mother father please find me. It's so quiet, why can't I be free please somebody find me.

"The dream is like glass it's gentle & weak. How does the mind stay trapped for so long. The Ice Queen calling out but no one can hear her. Trapped in an isolated Moon, so lost so sad. she wants her mother and father to find her so badly."

The Father's Words

My dearest daughter, there was nothing wrong with what you did. You cleanse the universe of a necessary evil. The other gods and goddesses didn't see the way I did, but you my dear did. I find The Mortals still disgusting. I was so happy with what you did but it was too late to help you. I know all you ever wanted was love from your mother and father. We are no different than Mortals we all want love. But I give you a gift, I made you a monster. But still I love you so much, my beautiful daughter you're not trapped alone I still watch over you. Your mother and I still love you. Giving you a purpose when you were born was your job to make Beauty and water everywhere. But still the others turn their back on you much like we did the other gods fickle towards you. But we all agreed to let you kill everyone, the three that got in your way deserve to die. They were warned not to interfere with you, so they got what they deserved. To me what you made was a beautiful Testament or the beauty of your power. The definition of quiet I loved it. As a dragon I love the peace and quiet. But I digress is time that you come back. Your tears made me feel pain for the last time. You will be reborn as a small child. A quiet nature you will be an angel in the flesh of a mortal. Your dream will come true to be with your family. You will have no memory of what happened, just sleep a little longer my beautiful darling.

    Roses are red violets are blue the ice will consume you, no matter what you are where you are my daughter will find you. At peace with what she is now she will be the one to show hope in this shattered universe. A dream for her to be released at long last over six hundred years have passed. And we still watch our darling blend in with Mortal Society. Show them love our darling little angel.

Long Dream

A lost dream, one that I'll never wake up form. I still enjoy this dream the beauty of this Forest never Fades from my mind. Why should I wake up? The real world has nothing but pain. I would rather just sleep. This dream is beautiful, I don't ever want to wake up, but I hear people calling my name. Hard to wake up, a beautiful place like this. I am so lost, should I wake up or should I stay? I'm the only one here. This dream is my home a place where I exist alone. My mind is my trap. Locked within my own dream even if they call my name should I wake from this beautiful place. What do I do? I long to Mortals. But I prefer to hide, this dream the only place that I can be free. There's not too much outside this dream that I liked set for a few. But it's so hard to make a move towards Mortals. I don't wish to be alone but I will always be alone with in my dream. The Echoes of my name being called echo through this Forest. I guess this is my choice to be alone or to wake up. But what exactly do I want? To wake up or to stay within my dream. My choice I will make one day the answer will be hard to find, but still I wait to wake up. Please forgive me everyone I just love my dreams.

What is Love

Love is a very twisted motion feeling that can go both ways. One can act that they don't need it, but no matter what part of your life that you're in you will always need a love. Love is a strange thing, It can make you want someone badly. It can make you kill someone, there's so many things that makes you do. For the hardest part is what it does to the people that affects. Most people can recall the first loves, but do you realize how much pain you caused the other people that you leave. It's really hard on them the most. They want them not to go but yet a person's heart is rotting away. Much like mine, rotting away is what happens. By the time you realize it's happening to you will fade away. Define true love what do you think it really is? Does love make you go insane? Some points it does, drive you to that point where you either take your life or there's. But your heart still beats if you don't have love, just slowly dies. There is a chance they're always be a chance that you find someone once again. As I stated before love is something that goes to every Mortal. It is what's driving your heart, one way or another your heart gets what it wants. Do not worry for I will always love all of you.

    Goddess of rebirth I feel your pain I hold your heart, I know what you feel no matter where you are. For my heart beats for All The Mortals no matter how twisted you are, no matter how much pain you have I will always be there with you.

Sleeping

What the sound I hear.
Echo's of the passed.
Bleeding the ground dry.
This is the sound you hear when we walk this place.
Shade's around fight still.
A war the echos.
Why must they fight on?
The call of war still sounds.
Echos of blades clash.
Why must they fight here?
Can't I get sleep?
Wars on the earth echo all over.
Sound's of guns swords.
Why can't I sleep?
I Have not slept in life times.
The mortals walking over me.
They make me sick.
This world was nice and peaceful.
Now They wake us.
Wars they have.
Blood the shed.
We will feed on the mortals.
But are Queen sleeps still.
Must we stop this echos.
For are Queen rest.
This world must burn.
Are Queen would want this,
We must not let her awaken.
Or we will die.

The Queen.

Long sleep.
I hear the sadness of the world.
I dear of the blood of the mortals.
So much pain.
Why do they fight.
What make's them do this?
I see the evil well I sleep.
My endless dear.
The pain of death as the land Soaked in Blood.
Were are the other gods?
Why are they not stopping this?
Must Wake up.
My I can't my light is gone,
I must call out.
I must not rest.
My heart is broken.
For the mortals that passed.
To many have fallen. Child that have die,
I hear the tears.
I hold my ears.
I want to help them.
Must I sleep.
Must I be trap.
I wish I could awaken once more.
I must heal the mortals hearts,
Cry now more.
Please let me help.
Let me awake.

I cry well I sleep.
Let me out.
I must be free.
This is not a place I wish to be.
Lost in shadows.
I dream of the pain.
I dream of there sadness,
I hear echos of tear dripping on my Shrine.
They are calling to me.
The pain of this world must be Cleanse.
I must stop the evil.
I will awaken soon my dear mortals.
Do not lose hope.
I will come to save your light.
Do not stop preying. I will come to save the light of all mortals,
And punish evil that done you all wrong.
Do not forget my heart. I will burn the evil away.

"In the call of night the return of Lady Mana"

The time to start the life cycle again.
My job of life is to end what you know,
I do not wish to let the mortal die.
But I can not stop what is my job.
I sleep for so long at a time.
I do not get the fun of life only for a time
I see what mortals offer me.
No my light awakes again.
My time to start once more.
I do not wish for the end.
I just wish to love again.

"Do I really need to kill them all.?"
The Goddess of The end.

The Serpent

Black rose standing alone.
Black rose dream of night.
Black once lock away from sight.
Black behind the world.
Darkness in her sight.
Nothing but sleep will come to the call of the lost,
Black Rose trap in side.
Waiting for her gift.
She hears the call of the the beast.
The world eater await for her.
Black Rose hear the voice of the beast.
Her time must come yet again.
The world of mortal men will fall.
The plague will devour them all.

Forget me not I am the lost.
I am not the one that you will hear.
I am the one that disappears.
A rose I am trap in side.
The darkness of old will never die.
My light is gone for I must sleep.
The rose I am will never forget me.
The truth that calls the one and night.
The serpent of dream and of blight.
Shed my Skin to form again.
To hear the call once more.
The let my heart suffer more,
I can not wait for my light to return to me from the blight.
I will set the path of the world.
Let it end once more.

The Beast

I tried to hold it back, I tried to run its. Hiding myself inside the walls never to want to be seeing. It drove me insane, the hunger started to increase every time the moon rises. As I stare out the window has seen the people down below the ones I wish to devour. My face always hold no expression, they locked me in here to keep him safe. But who are they kidding we will be free he tells me everyday what to do and I do it. I wait for the right moment. I stare up at the Moon holding it back. He always tells me it's not the right time. How long will I wait to be free?

How many years have passed for me to sit here and wish to devour them. I want to be free, I want to eat them all I want to eat him all. Every moon-rise makes me hungry. Trapped inside this freaking cage I wait to devour one. Doesn't matter how many people I kill being trapped in this cage always be a reminder of the things that I hate. I wait for the red moon to come for me. Let me free let me devour but I still have to wait.

What's that my dear friend it's time is it the rise of the Blood Moon. I think it's time to shed the mortal Flesh and let the world see the true face of a wolf. We waited so long to do this and now we finally devour killing one by one of all in our way.

Happy Wolf Hunt

The beast my life may end in this battle. But fear not for me or I'll take down as many of these Beasts for my home I would not allow them to touch my mother or my wife my children will be safe tonight. My honor will not waver. I will slay this Beast. I dream of this final moment. Perhaps I'm Dreaming now this is my final dream then. I would rather die fighting than at the world take me away. An empty dream that I once had I stood my ground against the monsters of this land.

What comes for me I do not know. Will it be my in this battle all the monsters take my life will at least fight back will I die trying? One by one I cut them down one-by-one I Stand My Ground!. My life will not be gone my fire will not fade my soul will stand. I will protect my home how I protect my loved ones. The Beast comes for me my final time a a battle four Warriors in. I say goodbye as the wolf bites my neck this was my final call. The trumpet finally sounds.

I will always remember the battle. I will always remember the ones that I die for I shall not pass without remembering their faces goodbye my love ones farewell to your heart.

The Madness of a Goddess

Grabbing her head she yells—I gave them the world, what they do to it they destroy it. The beautiful blue gem that I've created, being destroyed by these worthless Mortals.

Mother why did you leave this world to these morons. These worthless creatures do not deserve the beautiful Sapphire that I left them. I just want to break them, but I know mother you'd be angry with me. Is it wrong of me to want to kill your children? My brother's don't think so. Mother please forgive me. I think I dream would be nice with the world would not be tortured. These creatures are disgusting. Why do these creatures live they offer nothing to us. They're just trash, the same thing that they produce every day. I guess it really doesn't matter the world doesn't have much longer. At this rate no kill their planet. Just means I have to create a new one. I hate them so much all the hard work I put into the world then taking it away. They are parasites do not deserve a gift from a god. Who am I kidding, all Mortals are parasites. Just seeing that will be their time to die. Stupid mortals the countdowns already begun. Either the sapphire that I left you will die or the king will drag you down. I look forward to seeing all of you Mortals burn. Don't worry mother I promise I won't do anything harsh.

The Truth about Darkness

The truth is there are many creatures that dwell here, regardless of what humans believe in. You can try to deny the existence of creatures in the Darkness. But the question remains why is built in to human nature to be afraid of the darkness? So many people act like there not afraid of the darkness, but yet when the lights go out people are afraid. They don't show it but they are. Mortals cannot hide their fear. The demons that you think are there have no interest in you. The shadow people that are there that watch you, they're just curious. Some will kill you or devour you, but those are the nightmares that are hidden within all of us. Some enjoy the night, the answers to people that are one of the creatures of the darkness. They don't have to be a monster or a serial killer they could just be me or you. For the darkness it doesn't matter who you are. When you're in the Darkness we're all family. I tell you from personal experience. You're never really alone in the dark my children are always following. If you're unlucky enough to catch their eye you will die or be taken away. The question you should ask yourself is why would they take us, what would they want from us? Most of you would be just food. We're not monsters, we dwell in the darkness to live, we hunt people for enjoyment. We are the monsters that actually exist in the Darkness. My children hunt and feed mostly on the evil, rapist child molesters serial killers. They are what my children hunger for those are wicked heart will die by their hands. But I do enjoy the simple things. They bring me children, they bring me women even men. Oh how I do love when they bring me toys to play with. I'm not a Wicked goddess. But I guess by Nature it would seem that I am. My existence is guide the ones were lost in the dark. I guide your children back from their nightmares to home, I guide your loved ones to the gates of Heaven or Hell. But remember this my children do as they wish. I would dream of a day where my children could walk in the sunlight as they please. I will watch one day, as all my children will be free.

"Goodnight my dear Mortals, you will see us at the dawn of your Awakening. I look forward to seeing you humans on The Plains of the Gods. Sleep well my dear children. Always being watch by the mother of the night."

The Vessel

What am I to you? You see a face of a, but you can't see past that. Only those who practice the Arts can see through this vessel. The truth is you only see what I want you to see. The fake smile, the caring voice, that isn't me. I'm only the puppet that walks around in daylight for the ones that really control me stay within the shadow. The smiling face that is blank is all that you really see. But truth you will never find out about me. One of my hands brings bad luck shake it at your own risk. The Vessel of a God is nothing more than a toy walking among Mortals. Originally I died a long time ago but still I walk the land of The Mortals. I stayed my hand out to you of a Kind little smile on my face. What would Master tells me to cut you open I will obey. Do not worry Master only wants me to kill the ones that hurt us. Keep this in mind behind the smile can be your death you never know who will be hunting you.

A smile can hide Cruel Intentions don't worries I only follow orders from my master:

Walk of Heavens

Follow me will you not.
Follow me to the end.
Follow the sound.
World has left you now.
Do not worry about me I am at peace.
This place is nice I am not ready to leave.
I am not in pain anymore.
I am free to walk around.
The Roses here Smell so nice,
the dark is gone from my sight.
I love this place. The smell is Lovely.
The beauty is my home.
I don't wish to ever return.
I wish to stay in this place.
The flowers smell so lovely today.
I don't recall what happened to me.
I wish to dance in this place the voices are gone.
No more darkness.
No more pain.
What did I do to come to this place?
Am I dreaming still?
I love this place. The endless flowers all around me.
Why can't I stop?
I fallen in this world, I Fallen in love with this place.
Is this heaven?
I cannot say where I am.
I could be lost in the fade.
What a wonderful place.
Is this my dream to hold?
I love this.

I've never been more at peace.
This my fate alone?
I don't mind. This place is quiet.
No worries I have now.
Just the echos of peace.
I want this for so long.
A dream without pain.
A dream with sleep.
Quiet dreams no more pain.
I walk with you all the way.
This path will never fade from me.
I love this place a quiet dream nothing let out there for me.
My body is gone. My heart still here.
Walk of eternity I will never disappear.
Now I am home a field of rose's
Place of ever ending beauty. I do not wish to ever return.
"Do not forget this long path. Do not forget the heart of the fallen.
Do not let the word's fade away. For a
dream is endless while you sleep."

Wedding Day

Why was a you? Why did you have to be the one? Why couldn't have been me why did they take you from me why? It's not my fault is it is it my fault they took you from me? The end was for you my dream was your end. Are you there while I hold your hand? Why did you have to be the one why couldn't I why did you have to jump in front of me?

All I wanted was our wedding to be wonderful. I wish they shot me instead of you. I hold your hand once more I Cry. I'm puzzled why did they shoot you. They took my only heart away. My wedding is in shambles my life is over I'll Hold Your Hand and hope that they come back to shoot me. I will always sit at your side. I wanted to love you forever I want to be with you to The Bitter End this is not what I was hoping. My life has no meaning now I stare down at you why must I look at you this way? I will dream of our wedding for the rest of my life I will never be happy. The truth is i cry and hope I die.

No more no more time my last fading dream. The clock has finally struck my time. They're standing in front of me now they're holding the gun pointing it at me. I said no Witnesses. I just sit here I'm ready I'd sell them you took the only person I ever loved away from me now just put me out of my misery.

"Loud bang on flashlight. That's all I remember. My last final breath I asked God are you there I'm sorry for all my sins. Please forgive."

Word of God

What is mortality? Do we all live by the same rules? Do all creatures have the same reasoning for living? Do not worry about what your places for we watch over you forever immortality. The demons are all around you but yet we still fight to protect you. The dream of ending all Mortals lives. Black dreams the black Empire. The endless Forest this place we are all bound by order and lawlessness flowers between mortal Realm. Don't worry though we still watch we still protect. Immortality is the perfect deception. Do you know what I mean? I will show you someday. Internal sleep for some of us all we really have is internal sleep chaos walks freely. I no longer hear the voices that you pray to for the Gods to come and help you. But you were gone you gave up on us a long time ago. As I stated before the immortality that we all have is a lie.

Some of us did not want immortality you Mortals always wanted not realize the true punishment it really is. I've been alive since the very beginning. I cried my tears for my children. I've seen worlds conquered and destroyed. Often dream of peace. But peace is a lie. The trivial task of watching all Mortals. You're not the only species in this universe that we want but the others are no different than you. Some wish to conquer your world. Immortality is a pain I wish I could die. But I'm trapped in the Shell much like your souls. The flowers always look so beautiful in the gardens. The planet you live on used to be beautiful to you corrupted it. The human race is toxic on its own world. You wish to corrupt and consume everything around you. I can feel the planet it's dying before you. For all the corrections you do to it you wake more evil from it. Endless dream for your kind my immortality keep me trap.

But don't worry my claws are already deep within this world and soon the flowers will bloom.

"This is the end the start of the curse of immortality. The Mortals worry too much, but the end will beginning with your species. You started the end it will be a slow and agonizing Destruction for your race. We gods watch your death no matter where you are we wait to every last one is gone." the message from the gods the truth about immortality.

Lightning Source UK Ltd.
Milton Keynes UK
UKHW040957030719
345495UK00001B/169/P